A Castle
at the Straits

by

Janie Lynn Panagopoulos

and Illustrated by

Laura Evans

Mackinac Island, Michigan

A Castle at the Straits

By Janie Lynn Panagopoulos
Illustrated by Laura Evans

Design by Group 230, Lansing, Michigan

Mackinac State Historic Parks
P.O. Box 370
Mackinac Island, Michigan 49757

Library of Congress Cataloging-in-Publication Data

Panagopoulos, Janie Lynn.
  A castle at the Straits / by Janie Lynn Panagopoulos ; illustrations
by Laura Evans.— 1st ed.
      p. cm.
Summary: At Michigan's Straits of Mackinac, eight-year-old Chester
quickly learns the importance of the "Castle at the Straits" and the
work he will help his uncles, the "wicki," or lighthouse keeper, and his
assistant, do there.
  ISBN 0-911872-83-3 (hardcover)
[1. Lighthouses—Great Lakes—Fiction. 2. Lighthouse keepers—Fiction.
3. Mackinac Island (Mich. : Island)—Fiction. 4. Michigan—Fiction.] I.
Evans, Laura, 1963- ill. II. Title.PZ7.P18855Cas 2003
  [Fic]—dc21
                              2003002225

First Edition
First Printing 5000 copies

Printed in the United States of America

A Castle
at the Straits

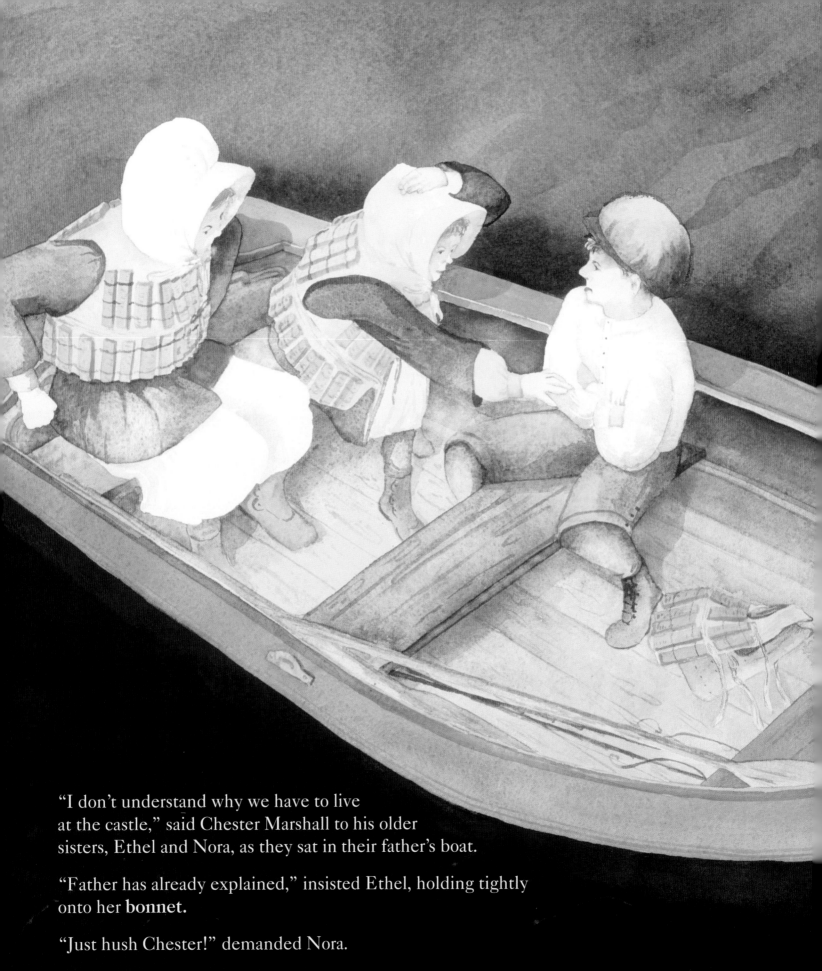

"I don't understand why we have to live
at the castle," said Chester Marshall to his older
sisters, Ethel and Nora, as they sat in their father's boat.

"Father has already explained," insisted Ethel, holding tightly
onto her **bonnet**.

"Just hush Chester!" demanded Nora.

Angrily, Chester stared out over the **Straits** of Mackinac.

Charles Marshall finished tying his boat to the dock and looked sadly down at his children. "I hope you know why I'm sending you here to live. It's time you get your education and Mackinaw Village is the best place for that. And Chester, it's time you worked with your uncles learning the **lighthouse** trade."

"I want you to know that each night as Uncle George lights that tower lamp, I'll be thinking of you, so you remember to think of me. Promise?"

Ethel looked away as she blinked back her tears.

"It's better this way, Papa," said Nora. "Because Chester will live with Uncle George and Aunt Maggie on the east side of the lighthouse and Ethel and I will be with Aunt Sarah and Uncle William on the west side. I think that's good," she said with a smile.

Chester looked at Nora and frowned.

"Time to go children," said their father, as he helped them from the boat with their **carpetbags.**

Standing on the dock, looking ahead, Chester could see **Old Mackinac Point** Lighthouse and knew why his father called it the "Castle at the Straits." It wasn't like any other lighthouse. Its tall tower and building of cream-colored bricks and red metal roof made it look like a castle from a book.

"Oh look at the daisies…" announced Ethel. "They're beautiful!" said Nora as she ran up the dock to the lighthouse lawn where a field of pretty yellow daisies grew. From above, a screeching party of sea gulls soared, following her.

"Blast those noisy birds. Rats with wings!" howled their father, shaking his fist in the air.

"Look! I look like a queen!" called Nora sticking a daisy in her hair and dancing around. Ethel and her father passed by Nora, ignoring her, as Chester stood on the dock and stared at his silly sister.

Just then, from above, a long chalk-white stream splattered across Nora's back onto her blue **Mackinaw coat.** Surprised, Chester didn't say a word, but smiled up at the screeching gulls.

"Ahoy!" called voices from the pillared porch. It was Uncle George and Uncle William; both had lived and worked at the lighthouse for many years. Uncle George Marshall was the old wicki, the **lighthouse keeper,** and Uncle William Barnum was his **assistant.**

"Ahoy!" called their father.

At that moment, Aunt Maggie, a short, plump, Irish woman stepped from the lighthouse, followed by Aunt Sarah, their father's sister. Aunt Sarah was short and thin, and always **proper.**

Aunt Maggie hugged Chester's father and the girls, greeting them. Chester smiled when Aunt Maggie pulled away, discovering the gift from the gulls.

Everyone laughed at Nora as Aunt Sarah and Maggie swished the girls into the lighthouse.

"Welcome Chester," said Uncle George.

"Come in son. Make yourself at home," said Uncle William, as he opened the lighthouse door.

From inside came wonderful smells of baked apple pie, roasted pork and biscuits.

"Oh me gosh!" cried Aunt Maggie as she wiped Nora's coat. "Look at Chester! Why I have to have a hug from such a handsome young boy." Aunt Maggie reached out her ample arms and pulled Chester close, giving him a smushy kiss on the cheek. Chester's ears turned red with embarrassment.

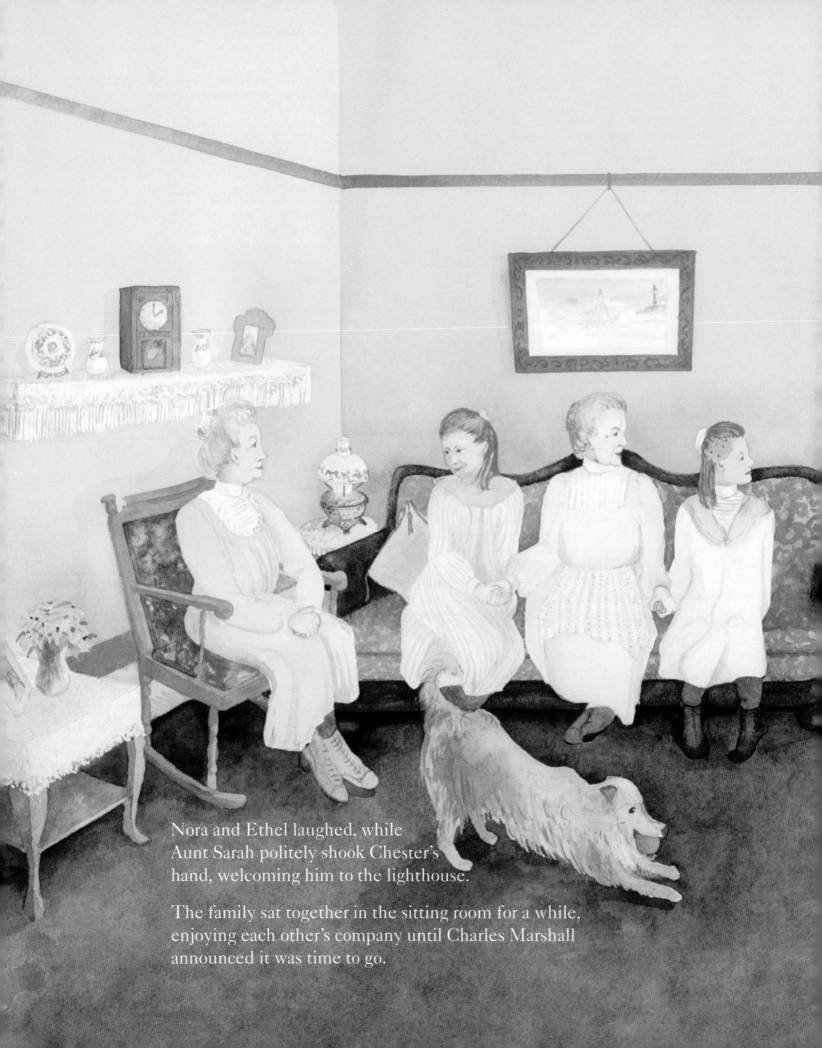

Nora and Ethel laughed, while
Aunt Sarah politely shook Chester's
hand, welcoming him to the lighthouse.

The family sat together in the sitting room for a while,
enjoying each other's company until Charles Marshall
announced it was time to go.

"Ya can't leave without supper," demanded Aunt Maggie as she disappeared into the kitchen.

"I best be shoving off... Girls, you mind your Aunt Sarah and Uncle William. Chester, listen and learn from Uncle George and behave yourself or Aunt Maggie will chase you down with her broom. I'll visit when I can. Remember, when your uncle lights the lamp, I'll be thinking of all of you."

"Yes sir," said Chester, as Ethel and Nora kissed their father good-bye.

"Don't you worry about the children, Charles. We have plenty to keep them busy," said Uncle George.

"Remember," said Charles, "Make sure they get their schooling come this winter. That's why they're here, to learn both books and the lighthouse."

"Wait!" called Aunt Maggie. "Here's supper, and don't let the gulls steal it or leave another gift."

"Rats with wings." howled Chester's father as he happily accepted the meal.

Chester and his sisters watched their father disappear down the dock, with the gulls soaring overhead. Ethel took a **hanky** from her pocket and dabbed her nose and Nora pulled the daisy from her hair, sniffing, fighting back her tears.

"Come girls," said Aunt Sarah. "We live on the west side of the lighthouse; let me show you your room." Uncle William picked up their carpetbags and followed.

"Would you like to see your room?" asked Uncle George, handing Chester his carpetbag and leading the way.

The lighthouse was large with creaky, wooden floors and steps, and tall ceilings. Chester's room had a metal bed and a window that looked down the beach. On a window shelf stood a collection of colored **beach glass,** the edges worn smooth by waves. There were also odd pieces of **driftwood,** and an Indian **arrowhead.**

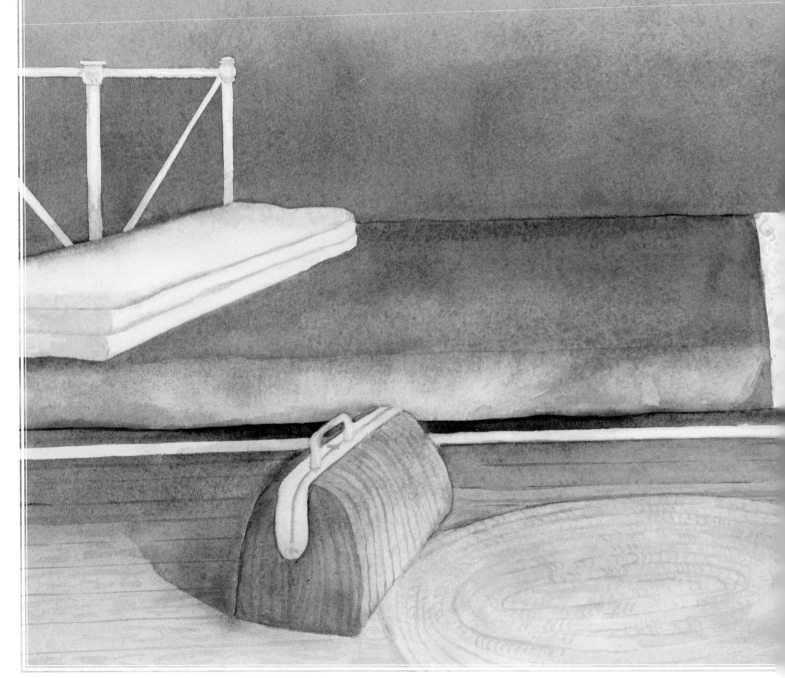

"Gifts from the Straits," said Uncle George. "All except the arrowhead, that's a treasure from the **old fort**. Maybe, if it's all right with your aunt, you can eat early and run down the beach to the **ruins**. Would you like that?"

Chester shook his head "Yes."

"But you must be back before sunset, to help with the light. That **lantern** is lit every evening, put out every morning, and cleaned in between; the sailors count on us. It's shined here since 1892, and is still winking-and-blinking its red eye out over those waters for safety."

"You promise to be back before sunset?"

"I promise!" agreed Chester.

Soon, Chester was eating potatoes, roasted pork and biscuits filled with sweet yellow butter.

"Chester!" snapped Aunt Maggie. "Slow down, chew your food and close your mouth when chewing!"

"Oh Maggie, the boy's only eight, he's excited. He wants to explore the fort."

"Fort or no fort, he'll use manners or be eating with the gulls. I still think he should wait for his sisters."

"Sorry, Aunt Maggie," said Chester. "May I be excused?"

"Excused? You've only just…"

"You're excused," interrupted Uncle George. "Remember your promise."

Uncle George smiled at his wife, patting her hand as Chester dashed out the door.

Outside, the sun hung low as Chester ran down the beach towards where old Fort Michilimackinac once stood. Above, gulls chased after him as the blue-green waves with white foamy hats splashed at his boots.

Soon Chester found a clearing where the dark pines parted way to an open space of blowing sand and leaves. There stood a few burned posts left from the old fort's walls. "This must be it!"

Falling to his knees, Chester began to dig for treasures in the sand. As he dug, the gulls gathered and the waves grew high. Soon, Chester noticed streaks of red and orange in the sky.

Standing, dusting sand from his knickers, he could see the sun starting to slide into the edge of the lake. Sunset!

Running back to the lighthouse as fast as he could, Chester dashed onto the pillared porch, stomping sand from his boots and throwing open the door.

"They're already on their way up!" called Aunt Maggie.

"You're late!" snapped Nora finishing her supper.

"You're in trouble!" added Ethel.

Chester yanked open the door to the lighthouse tower. It was cool and dark, and spiral steps wound round-and-round in the tower's belly. Taking steps, two at a time, Chester soon caught up with his uncles.

"You nearly missed it." snapped Uncle George. "The greatest thing a man can do, light the red winking-blinking eye of the Castle."

Chester caught his breath. "I. I…"

"No excuses." said Uncle William. "You just don't understand, but I'm sure after tonight you'll never be late again."

"Chester, you're a Marshall," said Uncle George. "That means you come from a long-line of wicki's, lighthouse keepers. It's a special job. Every day we keep a **log** of what happens here at the lighthouse, clean the light and **lens** each morning and trim the **wick** of the lamp."

"We battle the wind and the water to keep this light lit, and stay awake during storms, watching and tending the light, and sometimes rowing out into the churning sea to rescue **shipwrecked** sailors. Ain't that right, William?"

"Aye," agreed Uncle William. "The Straits are **treacherous** with waters running east and west, connecting the great lakes of **Huron** and **Michigan**. The Straits can go from glass-calm to rolling-churning **swells** as high as this tower, in minutes."

"That's true . . . " said Uncle George. "The only time it's calm is in winter, when the Straits freeze. That's why we don't light the red eye in winter. That's when you and your sisters will attend school at Mackinaw Village."

"But in early spring," added Uncle William, "the ice splits and huge chunks pile up along the shoreline. Ice so big it crushes **hulls** of ships. Why, if anyone counted, they would find 75 sunken ships on the bottom of these here Straits. This place is an 'Underwater Cemetery'."

Chester listened closely as he climbed the spiral steps.

Soon, they came to the top of the staircase. There, windows built into the bricks allowed the last rays of the sun to light the tower. They climbed a ladder at the center of the room into the **lantern room** above them.

"There she is… ain't she pretty?" said Uncle George.

Chester now stared at a great **prism** lamp. "She's beautiful. She looks like a jewel. No wonder she needs a castle to live in," said Chester.

"She's a **fourth-order Fresnel** with a red flash every ten seconds, making her wink at the sailors. She can be seen for 16 miles."

Uncle George walked the **platform** circling the lamp. "Chester, I want you to see something."

Carefully, Chester followed his Uncle, peering into the purple twilight of the Straits towards Lake Huron. Here, Chester could see tops of trees, a few houses, a church steeple from Mackinaw Village and then miles and miles of water.

"Look down, son."

Chester leaned against the railing and saw, standing below him, a red-brick building.

"That's our **foghorn**, powered by steam, fed by wood and coal, a job you'll take over. Feeding the **boilers** when **fog** is so thick a sailor can't see his hand in front of his face."

"It's an important job and the Marshall family is important to this lighthouse. You got to understand that you have the lives of men and women in your hands when you're a wicki. Especially here at the Castle at Old Mackinac Point."

Chester followed the windows around, looking out over the two great lakes, trying to imagine the many ships that passed the lighthouse, some carrying **iron ore** to build tall buildings or railroad tracks to cross the nation. Others, **lumber schooners**, carrying wood from sawmills on their way to build great cities in the west. And the **steamships**, filled with wheat, corn, and sugar beets, bound for the tables of America.

A lump came to Chester's throat as he thought about these things and how important it was to light the winking-blinking eye of the castle and feed the boilers of the foghorn. Being a wicki is an important job.

"A lighthouse is a symbol of America's growth," said Uncle William as he patted Chester on the back. "And it's our duty to always be here watching for the safety of others. Do you understand, Chester?"

Uncle George then reached over and opened a glass panel on the great lamp and removed a tall, red glass **chimney** from inside. Striking a match, he handed it to Chester. "Go ahead, young wicki, light the lamp."

Chester gently touched the wick of the **kerosene** lamp with the match while his uncles watched. Uncle George replaced the chimney and closed the panel, while Uncle William set the weighted clockworks of the revolving lamp in motion, making it move back-and-forth, winking-and-blinking its red eye.

The brilliant red beam cut across the purple sky, gleaming over the dark waves of the Straits of Mackinac. Chester felt a chill of excitement run up his spine, and remembered his father, thinking about him at the lighting of the lamp.

"Now do you understand, son?" asked Uncle George, his face painted red with light.

Amazed, Chester shook his head in agreement and whispered, "Yes." Now he understood.

Glossary

Arrowhead: pointed tip of an arrow

Assistant: a helper next in line for management

Beach Glass: glass that has surfaced from the bottom of a lake, ocean or sea and is polished by the surf and the sand

Beacon: a fixed aid to navigation

Boiler: a tank in which water is heated into steam

Bonnet: a hat with strings that tie under the chin

Carpetbag: a traveling bag made from carpet fabric

Chimney: a structure carrying off smoke from a fire

Driftwood: wood washed ashore

Fresnel Lens: a lens developed by Augustin Fresnel (Fruh-nell) using a series of glass prisms that greatly concentrated the light beam and made it visible for miles

Fog: a thick mist that is difficult to see through

Foghorn: a sounding instrument for warning ships in the fog

Fourth-Order: Fresnel lenses came in seven different sizes, first-order being the biggest; a fourth-order lens was about three feet tall

Hanky: Handkerchief

Hull: the basic frame of a ship

Iron Ore: stones from which iron is produced

Kerosene: a fuel oil distilled from petroleum

Lake Huron: one of the Great Lakes, flows from the Straits of Mackinac to the Detroit River, divides Michigan and Canada

Lake Michigan: one of the Great Lakes, flows from Chicago to the Straits of Mackinac, divides Michigan and Wisconsin

Lantern: a transparent case for shielding light and protecting it from the wind

Lantern Room: a room at the top of a lighthouse, usually surrounded by glass where the lighting apparatus of a lighthouse is housed

Lens: a piece of glass or glass-like substance that is used to focus rays of light.

Lighthouse: a lighted **beacon** of importance often with an attached dwelling for a lighthouse keeper

Log: a detailed record

Lighthouse Keeper: the manager of a tower or structure containing a beacon light to warn or guide ships

Lumber Schooner: a type of sailing ship with two or more masts that carries wood cut for building purposes

Mackinaw Coat: a short, felted wool jacket

Old Fort: in this case, Fort Michilimackinac, built by the French in 1714, taken over by the British in 1760, partially moved to Mackinac Island between 1779 and 1781; the remainder was demolished

Old Mackinac Point: located east of old Fort Michilimackinac directly across from the narrowest width of the Straits of Mackinac

Platform: a raised, flat surface

Prism: a transparent body of glass that breaks up light

Proper: correct in behavior

Ruins: the remains of something decayed or destroyed

Shipwreck: the destruction of a ship by a storm or collision

Steamship: a vessel driven by steam

Straits: a narrow stretch of water connecting two seas or lakes

Swells: large rolling waves

Treacherous: dangerous

Wick: a length of thread or rope in an oil lamp from which the flame is kept supplied with melted grease or fuel

Mackinac State Historic Parks

Although A Castle at the Straits is a make-believe story, the people and places in it are real. A fog signal began operating at Old Mackinac Point in Mackinaw City, Michigan in 1890. The "castle" lighthouse and keeper's dwelling were finished in 1892 and used until 1957, when the opening of the Mackinac Bridge made the light unnecessary. You can see the lighthouse and 1907 fog signal building in Mackinaw City today.

Our story is based on the family of George Marshall, who served as keeper at Old Mackinac Point from 1890 until 1919. He and his wife Margaret took in their nephew, Chester Marshall, when Chester's mother died in 1908. Chester's father, Charles, was a keeper at nearby St. Helena Island Station. Chester's sisters, Ethel and Nora, were raised by the assistant keeper at Old Mackinac Point, William Barnum, and his wife Sarah. Sarah was George and Charles Marshall's sister.

In 1895, six years after the creation of Old Mackinac Point Light Station, the Mackinac Island State Park Commission was established to care for Michigan's first state park. In 1909 the commission was given Michilimackinac State Park, which surrounded Old Mackinac Point Light Station. In 1958 the commission began a professional museum program, including reconstruction of Fort Michilimackinac. The commission purchased Old Mackinac Point Light Station from the federal government in 1960 to ensure preservation of the lighthouse. The lighthouse was opened to the public as a museum from 1972 to 1990, when it was closed due to budget constraints and restoration needs. Maintenance of the light station and research continued.

A fund-raising effort and restoration plan began in 2000. The fog signal building opened as a lighthouse information center with the original Fresnel lens from the tower on exhibit. Work continues on restoration of the structures and site thanks to grants, donations and income from the information center.

Care of Old Mackinac Point is a part of the museum and preservation programs operated by the Mackinac Island State Park Commission and known as Mackinac State Historic Parks. Museums and programs at Fort Mackinac and the Downtown Historic Buildings on Mackinac Island and at Colonial Michilimackinac and Historic Mill Creek on the mainland make the Straits of Mackinac one of Michigan's most popular travel destinations, and a wonderful place to learn about Michigan heritage and enjoy the natural beauty of the state.

For 40 years the Mackinac Island State Park Commission has preserved Old Mackinac Point. Decades of historical research by commission staff was used by Janie Panagopoulos in writing this book and by Laura Evans in creating the illustrations. We thank all involved for their fine work. We hope this book inspires new generations to preserve, understand and appreciate the maritime heritage of the Great Lakes State.

Carl R. Nold, Director

Mackinac State Historic Parks